Good Neighbor Nicholas

Virginia Kroll

illustrated by **Nancy Cote**

Albert Whitman & Company, Morton Grove, Illinois

For Abby, Ben, and Andi Pyne, who are very good neighbors.—V.K.

To my good friend and neighbor Joanne Friár, who is always there for me.—N.C.

The Way I Act Books:

Cristina Keeps a Promise • *Forgiving a Friend* • *Good Neighbor Nicholas*

Honest Ashley • *Jason Takes Responsibility* • *Ryan Respects*

The Way I Feel Books:

When I Care About Others • *When I Feel Angry*

When I Feel Good About Myself • *When I Feel Jealous*

When I Feel Sad • *When I Feel Scared* • *When I Miss You*

Library of Congress Cataloging-in-Publication Data

Kroll, Virginia L.
Good neighbor Nicholas / written by Virginia Kroll ; illustrated by Nancy Cote.
p. cm. — (The way I act books ; 5)
Summary: When Nicholas's injured ankle keeps him from playing soccer, he finds he can better understand the behavior
of the neighbor who makes him angry, and learns that he can change his own behavior, too.
ISBN-13: 978-0-8075-2998-0 (hardcover)
ISBN-10: 0-8075-2998-2 (hardcover)
[1. Neighbors—Fiction. 2. Behavior—Fiction. 3. Empathy—Fiction.]
I. Cote, Nancy, ill. II. Title. III. Series.
PZ7.K9227Goo 2006 [E]—dc22 2006000001

The design is by Carol Gildar.

For more information about Albert Whitman & Company, please visit our web site at www.albertwhitman.com.

Nicholas was angry. Nicholas was boiling. Nicholas was ready to explode! His neighbor, Mr. Robinson, was at it again.

Last Tuesday, when Nicholas was practicing soccer kicks,
Mr. Robinson had barked, "Keep that ball out of my roses!"

On Wednesday, when Nicholas's sister, Nina, was doing her dance routine, Mr. Robinson had phoned and said, "Can you turn that noise down a few notches? The bass hurts my ears."

Nicholas said to Nina, "I might as well forget about doing school band next year. I'd never be able to practice with *him* next door."

But Thursday was the worst. When Nicholas came home after school, his tiny dog dashed out the minute he opened the door. No one had been home since morning, and Bitsy really had to go!

"Oh, no!" Before Nicholas could stop her, Bitsy darted right next door. Nicholas gulped and chased after her. Of course, Mr. Robinson was in his rose garden.

It didn't matter that Nicholas said, "I'm so sorry, Mr. Robinson," or that he cleaned up after Bitsy. Mr. Robinson yelled, "There are leash laws in this town, you know. Next time I'll call the dog warden and have him take that beast to the pound, you hear?"

Nicholas swept Bitsy into his arms and ran back home. He slammed the lid on the trash can and banged the door behind him.

He was still angry when Dad came in.

"Sorry I'm late," Dad said. "Hey, what's wrong, Nicholas?"

Nicholas spilled out the story. Instead of being angry, too, Dad said, "Mr. Robinson has been very lonely since his wife went to live at the nursing home. He's old, and his back bothers him—"

Nicholas interrupted. "So what? He has no right to tell us what to do."

"He sure doesn't," Nina added. "He's just a mean old man."

Dad said, "Kids, sometimes people get grumpy when they're sad or in pain. And Mr. Robinson's wife loved those roses. He just wants peace and quiet."

"That's not our problem," Nicholas argued.

"I know it's not always easy to deal with Mr. Robinson," Dad said. "But you have to try."

The next week, Nicholas had one of those days when nothing went right. Dad and Mom had early meetings, so Nina had to get him off to school. "They forgot my lunch money," Nicholas complained.

"Let me make you a PB and J sandwich, okay?" said Nina.

"But I hate crunchy peanut butter," Nicholas said. "I'll borrow from my piggy bank." As he reached for his pig, he dropped it, and it cracked into pieces.

At school, Miss Kaney gave a surprise science quiz, and Nicholas got four wrong answers.

Then he twisted his ankle in gym, and Dr. Herman said, "No soccer for a week."

Nicholas was upset. Nicholas was sad. Nicholas was utterly miserable!
He sulked on the couch with his foot propped on pillows.

"Do you want anything, Nick?" Dad asked.

"I want to play soccer," Nicholas grumbled.

Nina said, "I'm sorry about your ankle, Nicky. Does it hurt much?"

"No, it tickles; what do *you* think?" Nicholas hissed.

"Well, excuse me for caring," Nina said. Nicholas noticed her and
Dad roll their eyes at each other.

Bitsy leaped onto his belly and licked his face. "Get down," Nicholas ordered, nudging her off. Bitsy slunk away with her tail between her legs.

Nicholas felt like crying. He hadn't meant to hurt Bitsy's feelings—or Dad's or Nina's, either! But he just couldn't help it. Everything had gone so wrong.

Nicholas glanced out the window and saw Mr. Robinson lugging out his trash cans and rubbing his back all the way down the driveway. Suddenly Nicholas realized, *I'm acting just like Mr. Robinson.*

Nicholas called Bitsy over. She hesitated for a moment, then jumped up and nuzzled Nicholas like always. "I'm sorry, girl," he whispered in her ear. Then he apologized to Dad and Nina, too.

Nicholas's ankle healed well, and soon he was good as new. Nicholas rode his bike, and Mr. Robinson yelled, "Keep those wheels off my lawn."

"I will. No problem, Mr. Robinson." Nicholas waved.

When Bitsy needed to go, Nicholas leashed her so she couldn't trespass on Mr. Robinson's property.

On garbage night when Mr. Robinson was gone, Nicholas took his trash cans out for him. After school, he returned the empty cans to the side of Mr. Robinson's house. He did that for several weeks in a row.

One evening just before dinner, someone knocked at the door. "Nicholas, could you get that, please?" asked Dad as he mashed potatoes. Bitsy followed, yipping up a storm.

Nicholas's jaw dropped when he saw that it was Mr. Robinson.

"Uh, hello," he said to Nicholas. "I came by to thank you
for helping me out. My back thanks you, too." Nicholas saw
a hint of a smile on Mr. Robinson's face. "You sure are a good
neighbor, Nicholas. You could teach me a thing or two about
being a better one." Mr. Robinson offered his hand, and
Nicholas shook it warmly.

Then Mr. Robinson reached into his pocket. "My niece owns a pet food store," he said. "Here, some healthy treats for your pooch."

At the word "treats," Bitsy yipped. Mr. Robinson and Nicholas laughed together.

"You're a good neighbor, Nicholas,"
Mr. Robinson said again. He was still
smiling when he reached his yard.
Nicholas was, too.